ALEXANDER GRAHAM BELL

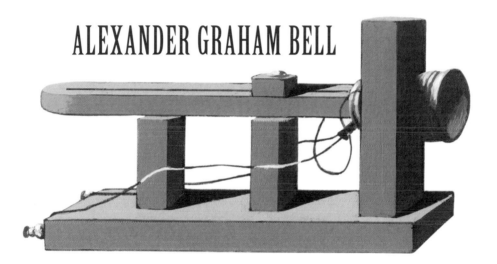

ALEXANDER GRAHAM BELL

by Leonard Everett Fisher

ATHENEUM BOOKS FOR YOUNG READERS

CHRONOLOGY OF ALEXANDER GRAHAM BELL (1847-1922)

1847	Born in Edinburgh, Scotland
1862	Studies in London with grandfather, Alexander Bell
1863-1866	Teaches music and speech in Elgin, Scotland
	Appointed Master of Weston House Academy, Edinburgh
	Experiments with electrically produced vowel sounds
1866-1868	Studies at University of Edinburgh
	Joins the university faculty
1868	Family moves to London, England
1869	Enrolls in London's University College
1870	Family emigrates to Ontario, Canada
1871-1873	Opens Boston school for teachers of the deaf-mute
	Becomes professor of speech at Boston University
1875	Produces sound electrically
1876	Receives U.S. patent for telephone
1877	Marries Mabel Hubbard
	Bell Telephone Company founded
1880-1889	Experiments with photoelectric cells and sound waves
	Invents metal detector, phonograph devices, artificial breathing device
	Introduces Anne Sullivan to Helen Keller
1882	Becomes a United States citizen
1890	Establishes American Association to Promote Teaching Speech to the Deaf
1895	Creates the tetrahedral structural unit
1898-1904	Appointed a regent of Smithsonian Institution
	Helps establish the Smithsonian's astrophysical observatory
	President of the National Geographic Society
1907	Sponsors founding of Aerial Experiment Association
1922	Dies in Nova Scotia, Canada

Atheneum Books for Young Readers
An imprint of Simon & Schuster Children's Publishing Division
1230 Avenue of the Americas
New York, New York 10020
Copyright © 1999 by Leonard Everett Fisher
All rights reserved, including the right of reproduction in whole or in part in any form.
With appreciation to Elliot Sivowitch, Museum Specialist, Smithsonian Institution

Book design by Nina Barnett
The text of this book is set in Galliard.
The illustrations are rendered in acrylic paint.

First Edition
Printed in the United States of America

10 9 8 7 6 5 4 3 ?
Library of Congress Cataloging-in-Publication Data
Fisher, Leonard Everett.
Alexander Graham Bell / Leonard Everett Fisher.—1st ed.
p. cm.
Summary: A biography of the prolific inventor who had a keen interest in voice and
sound and who worked tirelessly on behalf of deaf people.
ISBN 0-689-81607-3 (alk. paper)
1. Bell, Alexander Graham, 1847-1922—Juvenile literature. 2. Inventors—United
States—Biography—Juvenile literature.
[1. Bell, Alexander Graham, 1847-1922.] I. Title.   TK6143.B4F57   1998
621.385'092—dc21   [B]   97-32217

TO MY GRANDSON
MICHAEL STEVEN
WITH LOVE
—L. E. F.

DIAGRAMS FOR THE TELEPHONE PATENT
JANUARY/FEBRUARY 1876

"Be it known that I, ALEXANDER GRAHAM BELL, of Salem, Massachusetts, have invented certain new and useful Improvements in Telegraphy . . . My present invention consists . . . of a method of, and apparatus for, producing electrical undulations upon the line wire."

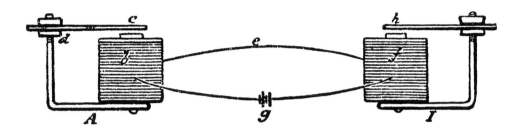

Witnesses:

Ewell & sick.

W. T. Hutchinson

Inventor:

A. Graham Bell

by atty Pollok & Bailey

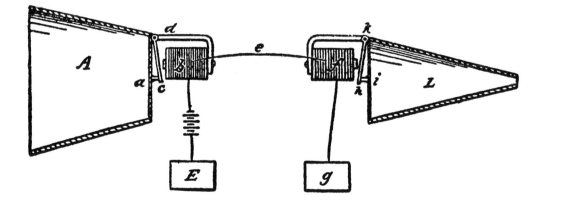

Witnesses

Ewell & sick.

W. T. Hutchinson

Inventor:

A. Graham Bell

by atty Pollok & Bailey

Nineteenth-century Edinburgh, Scotland, was the center of Scottish culture. Home to one of the world's oldest universities since 1583, Edinburgh spawned the romantic literature of Sir Walter Scott; the economic ideas of Adam Smith; and major studies in the medical sciences. The city's symbol, Edinburgh Castle, perched on craggy Castle Rock, recalled ancient Greece's Parthenon atop the Acropolis in Athens. So immersed was the city in learning that Edinburgh was called the "Athens of the North."

Among the brightest intellectuals of the city were the Bells. Alexander Melville Bell, like his father, Alexander, taught speech at the university and coached politicians to use their voices with style. They believed that clear speech was the mark of learned and civilized people. Their interest in speech mechanics and compassion for those born with speech disabilities led them to work with the deaf-mute.

One of Alexander Melville Bell's three spirited sons, Alexander Graham—"Graham" to family and friends—was born in Edinburgh on March 3, 1847. He was destined to dazzle the world of science and invention.

Graham's mother, Eliza Grace Symonds, was a painter and, despite partial deafness, a fine musician, a skill she passed on to Graham. Graham learned the piano with such relish and sensitivity that the promise of a career on the concert stage loomed large in his young life. But his enthusiasm for music did not include school, which he found boring. He preferred to roam the heather-covered fields of Corstorphine Hill. There, high above the coal-smoke haze that hung over Edinburgh's New Town like a grimy damp blanket, he had clear views of the sky and distant sea. And there, with excitement, he wondered about the motion of the sea, the essence of sound, and birds and the nature of flight.

ILLUSTRATIONS of VISIBLE SPEECH

[ENGLISH ALPHABET OF VISIBLE SPEECH,
Expressed in the Names of Numbers and Objects.]

[Pronounce the Nos.]	[Names.]	[Name the Objects.]		[Name the Objects.]	
1.					
2.					
3.					
4.					
5.					
6.					
7.					
8.					

[EXERCISE.]

One by one.

Two or three.

Four at once.

Five o'clock.

Half-past six.

Seven-thirty.

Eight to nine.

Ten or twelve.

Twice two, four.

Twice three, six.

Four and four, eight.

Nine and two, eleven.

Twice or thrice.

Two, a couple.

Twelve, a dozen.

Twenty, a score.

A book-case.

A few books.

New book-shelves.

A silver watch.

A gold watch.

The watch-key.

A good saw.

Cap and feather.

Tongs and shovel.

Sugar-tongs.

A hunting whip.

A table lamp.

A bunch of onions.

Corns and bunions.

A ship's boat.

A sailing boat.

Cart and horse.

A round tent.

Rows of houses.

A dog kennel.

A little monkey.

A pretty cage.

A green canary.

Between 1862 and 1863, Graham's education was entrusted to his grandfather, Alexander Bell, who lived in London, England. Under his watchful eye, fifteen-year-old Graham became consumed by the family's interest in using the human voice to communicate clearly.

Almost twenty years earlier, on May 24, 1844, American artist Samuel Finley Breese Morse had translated an alphabetic code into electric impulses and sent the message "What hath God wrought" from one end of a wire to the other. Many wondered whether the human voice could be transmitted the same way. Young Graham, among others, dreamed of replacing Morse's click-coded transmissions with actual transmission of the human voice.

Returning home, Graham and his older brother, Melville, tried unsuccessfully to produce vowel sounds over an electric wire. Graham continued to experiment at a school in Elgin in northern Scotland, where he was a student and part-time speech and music teacher, and at the Weston House Academy near Edinburgh where he later taught.

By 1866, nineteen-year-old Bell had enrolled at the University of Edinburgh, where his studies included the anatomy of the human voice box and ear. So expert was he in these studies that he was appointed to the university's faculty. As Graham studied and experimented with vibrating piano tuning forks, batteries, electrical current, and telegraph wires, his father perfected a voice-teaching system called "Visible Speech." Using a set of diagrams, he showed deaf-mutes, who had no idea of sound and thus could not conceive of speech, how to use their tongue, lips, and vocal chords to speak.

These lectures took the Bell family to London, where Graham worked with the deaf-mute alongside his father. There, he enrolled in London's University College to learn more about the anatomy of speech. And he continued his experiments, trying to make electricity produce vowel sounds.

The years 1868-1870 proved to be a time of triumph for the Bells. "Visible Speech" had become recognized as a vital tool in helping the deaf-mute to speak. When the elder Bell was invited to North America to describe his methods, Graham stayed behind and continued his father's lectures in London. But not long after his father returned, tragedy struck.

Graham's younger brother, Edward, and his older brother, Melville, died of tuberculosis. The dreaded disease lurked everywhere in the damp, sooty air of the British Isles. Invited to lecture in Boston, Massachusetts, in 1870, Alexander Melville Bell, not willing to suffer another shocking loss, packed up his remaining family and emigrated to Ontario, Canada. Although the Boston area seemed like a more logical place for the Bells to make their new home, they preferred the cleaner air of Canada and life among Scottish friends at Brantford, some sixty-five miles west of Niagara Falls.

Not long after Alexander Melville Bell and family settled into their new home in Canada, Graham, now twenty-four years old and called "Aleck," was sent to Boston in his father's place to introduce Visible Speech to the students of the Boston School for Deaf Mutes.

Bell was so drawn to the hearing-impaired youngsters of Boston that he remained to establish a school for the teachers who worked with them. He would later write, "My interest in the deaf is to be a life-long thing . . ."

Aleck's expertise as a teacher of speech and as a demonstrator of his father's Visible Speech system quickly established his reputation in the Boston region. In 1873, two years after arriving in Boston, Aleck joined the faculty of Boston University as a professor of vocal physiology, teaching courses in the biological science of the human voice—how human sound is activated. Teaching and lecturing during the day, returning to Canada during the summer months, the tireless Bell continued at night to experiment with transmitting sound over a single electric wire.

Aleck made no attempt to hide from others what he was trying to invent. His feverish effort to produce what would be called a telephone led him to consult the leading scientists of the day, including Joseph Henry, Secretary of the Smithsonian Institution, whose encouragement assured him that the invention of a telephone was not impossible. Aleck attended nearly every lecture in Boston that explained the science of electricity. He tinkered in the laboratories of the Massachusetts Institute of Technology and frequented the workshop of Charles Williams, Jr., a manufacturer of electrical equipment. There, he met and hired twenty-one-year-old Thomas A. Watson, one of Williams's skillful mechanics, to assist him with his experiments.

Aleck was moving closer and closer to creating a practical, working telephone. But he needed money to continue the work.

Thomas Sanders, a Boston businessman whose deaf-mute son, George, was one of Bell's pupils, saw the telephone as a major contribution to the advancement of business. He invested his savings in the project. Boston lawyer Gardiner Greene Hubbard became interested in Aleck, too, hoping that Bell could help his deaf daughter, Mabel. He visualized the telephone more as a money-making toy. But he, too, invested in the project.

On June 2, 1875, as Bell and Watson labored in the laboratory, a metal reed, one of several vibrating parts in the transmitting equipment Bell was tinkering with, became stuck. As Watson tried to fix the problem, he unknowingly set off faint undulating sounds that Bell heard at the receiving end of the connecting wire. These varying sounds recalled a vibrating piano tuning fork, a device that Aleck was very familiar with. In that one instant in which his wired gear made noises, Bell realized that he could convert sounds from a plucked reed into electrical equivalents of sound, send these equivalents along a transmission wire, and convert the signals back into sounds at the receiving end of the wire.

After some months of further experimentation, Bell wrote out an application to the United States Patent Office detailing the mechanics of what he had created. But he failed to submit it! Aleck had fallen in love with Hubbard's daughter, Mabel. He was too busy pursuing her to worry about the patent. Moreover, being that he was still a British subject, Bell preferred having a British patent and so put off his American application.

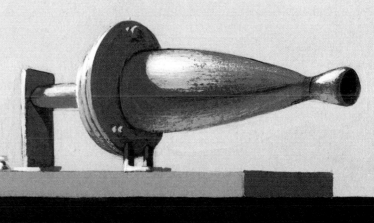

Mabel's father objected to Aleck's lovesick quest of his daughter instead of attending to the business in which he had invested. He became annoyed with Aleck's failure to submit the application for an American patent. While he did not think much of Aleck's invention, as a lawyer he believed it should be legally protected. Seeing that Aleck might never get around to it, Hubbard submitted the patent application himself on February 14, 1876.

"Be it known that I, ALEXANDER GRAHAM BELL, of Salem, Massachusetts, have invented certain new and useful Improvements in Telegraphy . . . My present invention consists . . . of a method of, and apparatus for, producing electrical undulations upon the line wire."

Two hours after the Patent Office received Aleck's application, it received a letter which began:

"I, ELISHA GRAY, of Chicago, in the county of Cook, and State of Illinois, have invented a new Art of Transmitting Vocal Sounds Telegraphically . . . I claim as my invention the art of transmitting vocal sounds . . . through an electrical current."

Elisha Gray claimed to have invented the telephone, too. But his letter just stated an idea; it was not an application for a patent. Gray offered no proof that his device existed, while Bell had almost a working device. On March 7, 1876, the Patent Office granted twenty-nine-year-old Alexander Graham Bell Patent No. 174,465 for the telephone.

It wasn't until three days after he had received the patent that Bell's telephone actually transmitted a human voice—his own. On March 10, 1876, Bell spilled some acid on himself. His assistant, Tom Watson, working elsewhere in Bell's house but connected to him by an electrically charged wire and a receiver, clearly heard Bell's call for help over the now-patented telephone:

"Mr. Watson, come here, I want to see you."

Bell's claim was fought all the way to the Supreme Court by several telegraph companies and crooked politicians, but to no avail. Even powerful Western Union tried to invent its own telephone. It didn't work. The Court would rule in 1893 that Bell invented the telephone.

Throughout this seventeen-year battle in the courts, Alexander Graham Bell was increasingly acknowledged as the leading figure in the advancement of electrically powered communication. The patent itself would become the most valuable patent ever issued by the United States.

On a steamy Sunday, June 25, 1876, the day General George M. Custer and his troops were wiped out at the Battle of The Little Big Horn in Montana, the newly patented telephone was demonstrated at the Centennial Exposition in Philadelphia to a small committee of judges. They cited Bell for his achievement. Among those on the committee was Elisha Gray, who, incidentally, was *not* among those who contested Bell's claim to be the telephone's inventor.

To the general public and its newspapers, Bell's telephone at first seemed like some kind of trickery. It wasn't until March 15, 1877, that Aleck Bell demonstrated his telephone publicly to two large groups of skeptical newspaper reporters and guests—one in Salem, one in Boston. Connected by a sixteen-mile wire strung between the two cities, they spoke to each other quite clearly. The reporters at both ends took notes as to what was said and later compared them. After that, there was no doubt that Alexander Graham Bell had changed the way the people of the world would communicate with each other.

In that same year, following his dramatic demonstration, Aleck founded the Bell Telephone Company, married Mabel Hubbard, and moved to Washington, D.C. Nine months later, on January 16, 1878, Aleck demonstrated his telephone for Queen Victoria of Great Britain.

Soon after Bell's success, advertisements for the telephone appeared in publications, such as this one that appeared in *Harper's Monthly*:

"A TELEPHONE Complete $3 guaranteed to work 1 mile. One guaranteed to work 5 miles $5."

By 1880, there were about 50,000 telephones in the United States, which then had a population of about 50,000,000. Approximately one in every 1000 people in the country had a telephone. By 1900, only twenty years later, the population of the United States had grown to a little more than 76,000,000, and 1,350,000 people—or one of every 56—owned a telphone. In the twenty-five years after Alexander Graham Bell had created the telephone, other inventors devised improvements to it that resulted in more than three thousand additional patents.

In the ten-year period 1880 to 1889, the suddenly wealthy Aleck offered considerable financial encouragement to others who showed promise in science and invention. In 1881, Bell backed physicist Albert Abraham Michelson's experiments with measuring the speed of light. Michelson would go on in 1907 to become the first American to win a Nobel Prize for Physics. In 1882, Aleck saved the bankrupt publication *Science* from extinction. The magazine would eventually become the official voice of the American Association for the Advancement of Science. Aleck was also generous to all institutions that helped the hearing-impaired.

And in that same year, 1882, he became an American citizen.

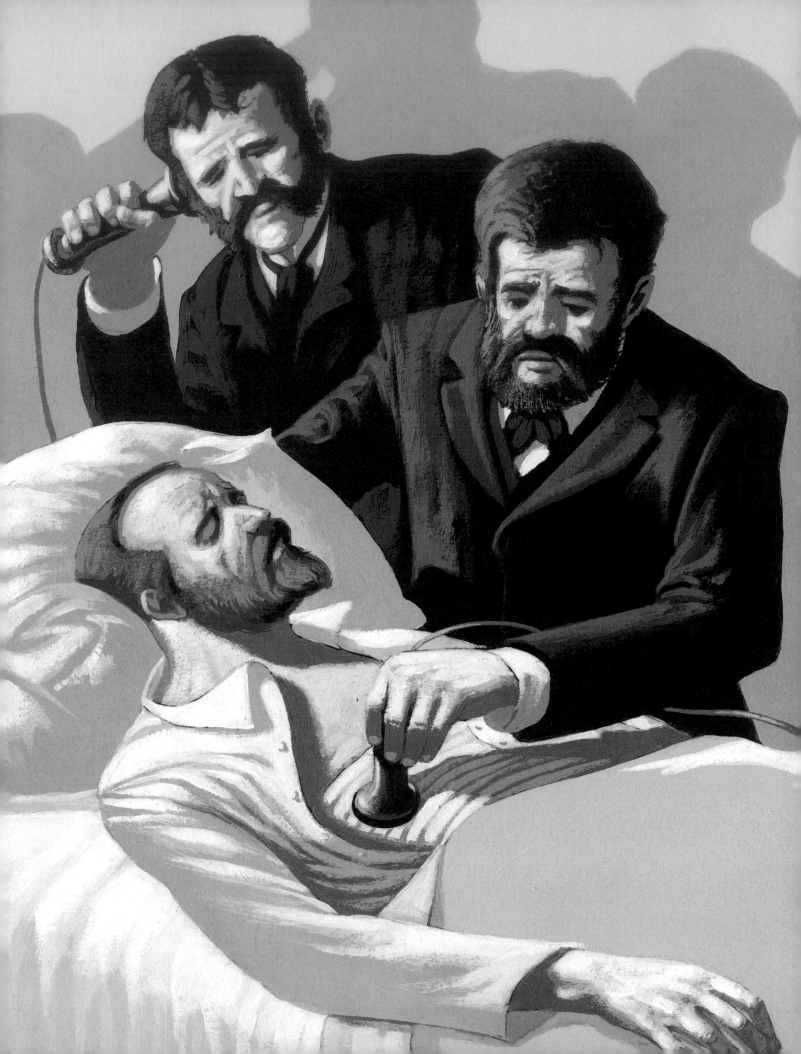

While generously supporting the scientific endeavors of others, Bell continued to busy himself with his own visions and new experiments. Sometimes a current event caused him to turn his inventive mind toward more immediate and practical needs. On July 2, 1881, a few months after taking office, President James Abram Garfield was shot in Union Station, Washington, D.C., by Charles J. Guiteau, a discontented office-seeker. None of the doctors called in to save the president could locate the bullet that was lodged somewhere in his midsection.

In less than four frantic weeks, Bell had devised a metal detector, the first of its kind, to find the hidden bullet. On August 1, 1881, Bell passed the detector over the president's abdomen. However, the device, whose sound changed when it came into contact with unseen metal at shallow depths, would not work properly. Perhaps the metal springs of the bed upon which the stricken president lay dying interfered with the electrically-charged probe. The bullet lay undetected. But it was too late anyway. Severe infection had already reduced the possibility of the president's recovery. He died on September 19th.

Disappointed but not discouraged, Aleck went on to perfect his metal detector. It was successfully used by surgeons before it was supplanted in 1895 by the X ray, discovered by Wilhelm Konrad Roentgen, a German physicist.

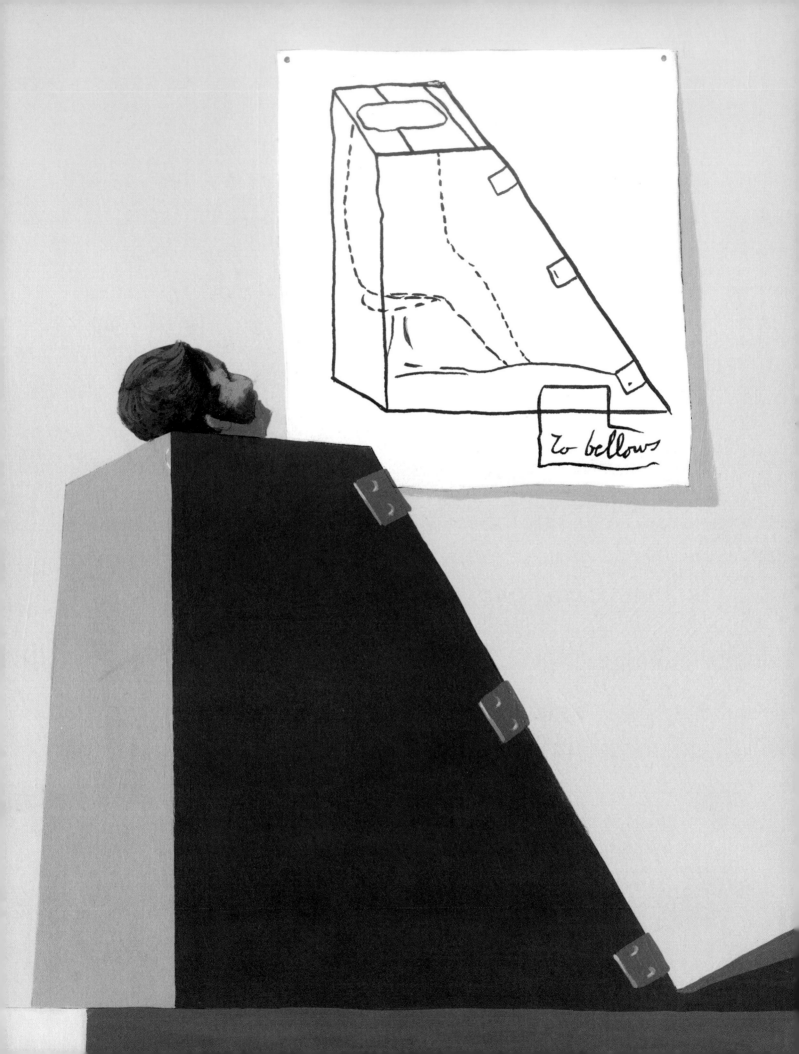

During the 1880s, Aleck's undaunted vision propelled him into other areas of practical science as well. He experimented with superimposing speech onto light waves—an idea related to modern fiber optics. This effort led to the "spectraphone," an instrument used to identify the chemical components of some substances, a process that later developed into the modern science called "photoacoustic spectroscopy."

Another of Bell's ideas was the "vacuum jacket," a device to help people with poorly functioning lungs to breathe. As President Garfield lay dying during the hot summer of 1881, Mabel and Aleck's newborn son stopped breathing and died. Aleck consoled his family, which now included daughters, Elsie and Marian (also called Daisy), and secluded himself in his laboratory. When Bell emerged from his work, he had a metal jacket that tightly encased the upper body of a patient whose lungs were not working properly. Attached to the jacket was an air pump that increased or decreased the air pressure inside. This enabled the lungs to expand and contract to provide air for a breathless person. The vacuum jacket predated by fifty years the construction of the "iron lung" to help polio patients breathe.

As time went on, Aleck's work, lecture, and travel schedule became fuller. His ambitions for himself, his family, and humankind in general kept him on the go morning, noon, and night, seemingly beyond human endurance. His joyous capacity for learning all there was to know about the universe grew as large as his waistline. Once a thin, rawboned young Scotsman, he had become a very corpulent American. But his personal indulgence was only matched by his compassion for those in lesser circumstances and by his generosity to those in need.

Among those who sought his help was Captain Arthur H. Keller, an influential Alabama newspaper editor. His daughter, Helen, had contracted a mysterious brain fever that left her blind and deaf before her second birthday. The only sounds Helen made were shrieks of hysteria accompanied by kicking and clawing tantrums.

In 1886, sensing that a sharp and clever mind lurked beneath the unintelligible outbursts of the deaf and sightless girl, Aleck introduced the now six-year-old Helen to twenty-year-old Anne Mansfield Sullivan, a teacher of the blind at Boston's Perkins Institute for the Blind. Anne agreed to try to teach Helen to read and write. That relationship endured for half a century. Helen graduated with honors from Radcliffe College and spent the rest of her life writing, traveling, speaking, and helping other deaf and blind people. Helen Keller remained ever grateful to Alexander Graham Bell, who became her longtime caring friend.

By 1890, Aleck divided his time between his Washington, D.C., home and a new summer retreat near Baddeck, Nova Scotia, Canada. He had already amply demonstrated his inventive genius and unselfish nature to the world. And the world had responded by showering him with honors, including a German honorary medical degree for his contribution on the functions of the human ear; France's Legion of Honor; and the Volta Prize, which had been established by Napoleon.

Aleck used the Volta Prize money to create both the American Association to Promote Teaching Speech to the Deaf, and the Volta Laboratory in Washington, D.C. The work at the laboratory involved the creation of electrical devices to assist the deaf. It led directly to Bell's improvement of Edison's phonograph and other devices in sound recording. Aleck contributed all of the income that came out of these Volta Laboratory inventions to help the deaf.

By 1895, Bell had turned his focus to the next forward-leaping invention after the telephone: mechanical flight. For several years he had backed Samuel P. Langley's flying experiments along Washington's Potomac River. Langley, Director of the Smithsonian, would not beat the Wright brothers in being the first to fly a "heavier-than-air machine," that is, a machine that did not use hot air or gasses to lift it off the ground. Yet he did contribute greatly to the development of flight.

On his estate in Nova Scotia, Aleck invented and experimented with huge tetrahedrons, or kites built out of multiple four-sided cells called "tetrahedrals," that were both light and strong. Bell's tetrahedral principle of construction would one day find its way into modern twentieth-century architecture.

Always the visionary, Bell was sure that mechanical flight was practical and close at hand. He wrote in 1896: ". . . it will be possible in a very few years for a person to take his dinner in New York . . . in the evening and eat his breakfast in . . . Ireland . . . the following morning."

In 1904, the Wright brothers flew an airplane for the first time. Bell, impatient to improve the flying machine, established the Aerial Experiment Association in 1907. However, instead of working on airplanes, Bell's group perfected an Italian invention called the "hydrofoil," a winglike apparatus designed to lift a boat above water to allow it to travel more smoothly and speedily on a cushion of air. Between 1919 and 1929, Bell's hydrofoil held a world speed record of 61.62 knots (70.86 miles per hour).

In 1898, Alexander Graham Bell was appointed a regent of the Smithsonian Institution. While at the Smithsonian, his interest in flight, the sky, and the star-strewn space above led him to create that institution's astrophysical observatory.

Between 1898 and 1904, he was president of the National Geographic Society, succeeding his father-in-law Gardiner Greene Hubbard, one of the magazine's founders.

As busy as he was exploring the world and everything in it, and trying to harness nature's powers while helping others to do the same, Aleck Bell never lost interest in easing the burden of the deaf-mute, the blind, and the ailing—most especially afflicted children. He was a familiar and affectionate figure among them. After visiting a school for deaf children, he wrote: "Some of the youngest children somehow got the idea that I was . . . Santa Claus . . . ! The children were much puzzled to know how so big a body could come down so small a chimney. I taught them the word 'squeeze'!"

In the twilight of his life, Alexander Graham Bell—Dr. Bell as he was now respectfully called—continued to enthusiastically embrace dozens of projects. Among these were the conversion of salt water to fresh water, sheep breeding, and the radio.

Dr. Bell died at his Canadian retreat on August 2, 1922. He was seventy-five years old. It is hard to imagine any scientist, inventor, or tinkerer more energetic, forward-looking, eager to please, and with more feeling for and generosity toward the less fortunate, than Aleck Bell.

Such was the man.